A Story of Blessing and Discovery

By Kathy Long
Illustrated by Joe Boddy

Augsburg
MINNEAPOLIS

HALLELUJAH THE CLOWN
A Story of Blessing and Discovery

Copyright © 1992 Augsburg Fortress

Scripture quotations unless otherwise noted are from the Holy Bible: New International Version. Copyright © 1978 The New York International Bible Society. Used by permission of Zondervan Bible Publishers.

ISBN 0-8066-2560-0   LCCN 92-70384

Manufactured in the U.S.A.   AF 9-2560

96 95 94 93 92   1   2   3   4   5   6   7   8   9   10

To Steve Williams
the real Hallelujah the Clown

He watched his group of friends. At first they looked surprised. Hal's singing was not exactly what they had expected. Then they started to laugh, and they laughed and laughed and laughed.

Hal was embarrassed. His face turned red, and the corners of his mouth turned down. He walked away, looking sadly at his feet. Hal was so sad that he didn't hear God say, "Good work, Hallelujah. Good work."

"Singing is not my thing," Hallelujah said, "but being a child of God is." So he did not give up.

Soon Hal saw another group of friends sitting in a circle. One of them was dancing. He jumped. He twirled. He dipped. Everything he did was wonderful.

Hal's insides tickled just watching him. His friends were all smiling, and Hal knew their insides tickled, too. Hal supposed even God's insides tickled, seeing this beautiful dancer.

Hal stood and watched the dancer for a minute. It looked like such fun. Then he got an idea.

"I bet I can do that. Maybe that's what I can do," Hal said to himself.

Then the corners of his mouth turned up and Hal smiled.

When the dancer sat down, Hal went to the group. He did a couple of leg stretches. Then he jumped. But something strange happened. Instead of landing on his feet, he fell down on his seat. Then he twirled. But he didn't stop. He twirled and twirled and twirled until he was dizzy. He flipped and he flopped. Then he stopped. Poor Hal.

At first, his group of friends looked surprised. They had never seen dancing like this. Then they started to laugh, and they laughed and laughed and laughed.

Hal's happy smile disappeared. He was so sad. The corners of his mouth went down again, and he walked away, looking at his feet. Hal was so sad that he didn't hear God say, "Good work, Hallelujah. Good work."

"Dancing is not my thing," Hal said, "but being a child of God is." So Hal did not give up.

Hal walked some more until he came to another group of friends sitting together. One of them was playing a lute. The melody was sweet, and the next thing Hal knew he was humming. In fact, all of Hal's friends were humming. Hal supposed even God was humming along with the beautiful music.

He watched the musician for awhile. It looked like such fun. Then Hal got an idea.

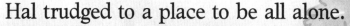

Hal trudged to a place to be all alone.

"Playing the lute is not my thing," Hal said. "I can't do anything right, no matter how hard I try."

A big tear ran down Hal's cheek.

For a minute, Hal was quiet. Finally, he could listen to God.

And God said, "Hallelujah, you are wrong. You did please me."

"But I can't sing," Hal said.

"No, you cannot," God said.

"And I can't dance," Hal said.

"No, you cannot," God said.

"And I can't play the lute," Hal said.

"That's true, too," God said. "But that's not why I made you."

"Why *did* you make me?" Hal asked. "Every time I try to do something for your glory, everybody laughs."

"That's why I made you," God said. "You bring joy to all my other children. That is a gift and it makes you special."

Hallelujah felt warm inside.

Then the corners of Hallelujah's mouth turned up, and they stayed that way.